Operation Jivundu

Operation Jivundu

SCRIBE'S QUEST

CHIMBA KABAYI

Copyright © 2020 by Chimba Kabayi.

Library of Congress Control Number: 2020914175

HARDBACK: 978-1-952155-70-3
PAPERBACK: 978-1-952155-69-7
EBOOK: 978-1-952155-71-0

All rights reserved. No part of this publication may be reproduced, distributed, or transmitted in any form or by any electronic or mechanical means, without the prior written permission from the copyright owner, except in the case of brief quotations embodied in critical reviews and certain other noncommercial uses permitted by copyright law.

Ordering Information:

For orders and inquiries, please contact:
1-888-404-1388
www.goldtouchpress.com
book.orders@goldtouchpress.com

Printed in the United States of America

Contents

Dedication vii
Acknowledgments ix
Prologue xi

Chapter 1 – The Beginning 1
Chapter 2 – The Confrontation 9
Chapter 3 – An Old Trail 19
Chapter 4 – Cracking The Puzzle 27
Chapter 5 – The Final Score 35

DEDICATION

For Mum, Dad and my Grandfather

Acknowledgments

Mrs. E. Chibende, Mrs. Dube for providing me with the Xlibris experience. Mr. D. Simfukwe, Mr. M. Mwiinga for their support and encouragement. Judith, Rita, Margaret, Annette for assistance rendered. Mr. Kapya for lending me his laptop to finish the novel. Most importantly my brothers Evaristo and Jonathan, my wife especially for her patience and diligence to bring this work to reality.

Prologue

In the world of reporting it is only virtue and good instincts that keep you going. That's what happens to two friends when they decide to join the world of scribes, people who are fearless to bring the truth to light.

This leads them to discover that they have more than so much in common. As they both discover that they have got estranged siblings and more follows them from history. Michael Fwando and Jake Chingu along with Vasco, Jack, and Virginia are the centers of this intriguing story.

With mercenaries on their trail after exposing them in the media. Michael and Jake must outwit their adversaries and stay ahead. However, after Jake's sister's murder, things change they get something more than they bargained for! Someone is hunting them and they have to stay ahead of him.

With the help of Vasco, they must expose and bring down the Banchili's, leaders of the mercenaries. Who are deadly because they leave no prisoners.

CHAPTER ONE

THE BEGINNING

Operation Jivundu

Ideas were racing in my mind, stuck with the guiltiness of letting my friend cover the story alone. His body badly wounded by bullets that hit him on the battlefield. To make matters worse he had lost a lot of blood due to excessive bleeding as he lay on the bed in the hospital. Narrating between sobs and gasping how he was caught up in crossfire which was going between a mercenary-like small army and the state army. All this happened in a small country called Bamvunde in a city called Manguvu. My friend battling for his life managed to give me patches of the information, word had it that an oilfield, an undeveloped goldmine, and some illegal dealings. These issues and a couple of heavens know what!! These events happened in just one month, I was covering two columns:

Have your Say and who's in charge.

But in the meantime let me take you back six years ago when Michael Fwando, that's me and Jake Chingu, my best friend had just finished college. I discovered that Jake and I had a lot in common- even our ambitions were a little similar. I loved writing articles; he liked reporting, digging for information, that kind of thing. But our first break wasn't anything to do with journalism. I was working for a cotton ginnery and my friend was working for a papermaking factory. This was right after high school. Then things suddenly began to change; I was a keen reader of the Blaze Daily newspaper. I developed an interest in writing articles to the editor in the people's column. Meanwhile, my friend was interested in gathering information from the local area. Working at the cotton ginnery wasn't really my area of interest, I knew to be in the papers or on TV was what thrilled me. As for Jake, he couldn't wait to start a course that involved reporting.

Jake and I were anxious so we began to look for people working either for electronic or print media. During this period we would roam the town and check press offices. Finally, through an old school mate, we found a link, his uncle, a sub-editor of a local paper. We told him about our concern and he listened with interest as he leaned forward each time our story got exciting. He told us to see him in two weeks, with our work, written articles even anything local. We continued working and saving money for college. Alongside we were now being coached by Mr. Vinji the editor on professional writing and reporting. That's how the foundation of our careers started. We were lucky right after our smalltime jobs; we were offered places for a job on training. We were attached to a newspaper called the montage, I was given a task of sub-editing and my friend into the reporting section but we could interchange. It took us about two years to gain experience and after that, we had a meeting with the chief editor. We were called to his office, and then he said, " gentlemen I got news for you". You both know that we won't need extra baggage.

"I have decided to offer you jobs, as for the others they have been laid off. So what you do say? We both replied thank you, sir, we are ever grateful. Mr. Bindwo just shrugged his shoulders I like helping young men with a passion for journalism. It was in the third year that we finally accomplished our goals, done with college, high school, and small jobs. We now began to work with the rest of the staff; I was working with the news setting and editing section. Jake was working with the reporters and foreign news section. I forgot to mention that reporting was also part of my job. Although I forgot to mention Jake had the same training as I did it's only that he liked the fieldwork more than me. Another thing I also could do was typesetting."

So continued our quest to become the best pair of scribes in the game. Due to Jake's persuasion, I secured a space in the local news section. This is the time when we encountered a lot of weird stories. There was this incident when a certain boy ate his father's meal. Upon returning from the fields he discovered what his son had done. He did even bother to ask his son but just clobbered him to unconsciousness. The boy died instantly when the police searched for him but he remained at large. So this was my story. Jake covered a more interesting story about a troop of cannibal monkeys. Word had it that there was hunger in the jungle and humans became the alternative food.

The humans were now being terrorized by the primates before the state moved in to crop the carnivorous creatures. These are the kind of stories we encountered in the early days as journalists. I must admit though doing what our dream work was fun, it also tedious work. I had to get used to it.

One day Jake and I had a conversation over what kind of stories he liked to cover. Michael, you know what? This local stuff isn't that exciting we have to go for the big things out there. We have got to know what's happening out of town, at the borders and beyond. What do you think? Well, I began; it is a good idea though it may take some time to get used to. So what are you saying, Michael? We drop the subject or what...! Mmmmh no, no, no you don't understand me, I mean we need leverage to come on Jake. Trust me on this one am with you all the way okay. Alright, alright Michael that's all I needed to know. I have already talked to Mr. Bindwo he said he will recommend us to the chief editor. The chief editor is Mr. Ngwiza I hope you know that Michael. So we will start this month.

During this time we covered stories together but I did most of the editing who's who the paper I later had two columns have your say and in charge. Jake had a more interesting column close talks and the iron fist. My column looked at people's views and management issues; Jake's column was dealing with government debates and power struggle in politics.

There was now stiff competition between the papers the montage my paper; flash newspaper and the blaze daily newspaper. It was from the blaze where we got our first training conducted by Mr. Vinji. This was the world of scribes and the game of who's who in providing information. There was a tale of cattle rustlers who had been terrorizing some commercial farmers in Ngaro.

According to sources, the rustlers had a habit of leaving the skull of a cow. On the entrance of the cattle kraal. These had now become a menace in the ngaro farm block. Farmers were not at ease they lived in fear of being robbed of their cattle. They had tried getting help from the police in the area. This only became a temporary solution as the cops didn't come for regular patrols. It took some time although the cases of rustling had lessened.

Finally, the paramilitary handled the situation and caught some of the rustlers. The paramilitary couldn't take in all the cattle rustlers, as the rest of them were killed in the gunfire. There were about ten of them but only four of them were nabbed one escaped. Firearms were recovered and lead as to be they sold their loot after raiding. They testified about their buyers and a lot of you know where stuff! This was a column by Michael Fwando of the montage.

There was also another incident in the coastal town of mondo in a country called mongalao. This country had a beautiful coastline near the sea about a hundred meters from the shore. The distance that long was the pirates were hijacking private yachts and the situation was getting out of hand. The gang was called the Panthers they either would hijack a yacht with passengers to get a ransom. Or they would get the yachts for ransom as well. The most surprising thing was that the criminals were being financed by a top official. This official was a government governor with a pseudonym the scarlet jaguar. The same thugs were connected to an international gang the condors. They had now covered a huge radius near the crustacean islands; the base was among these same islands.

This whole scheme was discovered by a private investigator with a few links to the government and another link of the inside information in the coral islands. The investigation began when the governor became a little twitchy; a certain businessman was being blackmailed. Following the traces of the sender of the information, they lead him to the Panthers and their financier. To his dismay, the financier was one of his business partners but the name scarlet jaguar wasn't familiar. It didn't ring bells. When Mr. Jerry Vangezi thought about the Panthers he was shaken they wanted ransom on his yacht. He paid up. He began to dig for answers just when he got close enough. So close to knowing who the scarlet jaguar was! he disappeared.

Chapter Two

The Confrontation

CHAPTER TWO

The Confrontation

Vangezi's disappearance caused a stir both in the media and in mondo. Even in Jerry Vangezi's city, Geovis everybody was wondering what could have happened. The local tycoon had just vanished into thin air. It wasn't long before the story reached the police then the government. After some raised concerns a case was opened by the Vangezi family. This is when the private detective sprung into action, he did his job. He just couldn't figure out who the scarlet jaguar was, however, the Panthers were exposed. Something had to be done about the situation.

Mongalao's marine police swung into action, they caught a handful number of the Panthers. They sweated them and one of them spoke up gave a few addresses and other details. He mentioned the financier's middle name Marseille, including his occupation. He spoke more about the crustacean islands its operations and the condors who were the buyers of the stolen yachts. The marine police couldn't gain access to the islands as they were privately owned by a foreign millionaire. Inter pol had to be involved this became a big fish to fry. Vangezi yachts provided private parties for the Panthers, condors, and businessmen. They conducted underground meetings every two months; money laundering, illegal gems deals, yacht selling and a lot more. All this explained Jerry Vangezi disappearance.

This has to stop said Marx Deveraux the private investigator. I just don't know how to stop it. Just for starters, Marx was an ex-military man, police detective, and intelligence attaché'. Deveraux was the main man on the Vangezi investigation. He managed to bust up a good number of the Panthers; the fourth in command was nabbed by the marine police.

Gwani better known as the bear was the one, Vaza Gwani and three of the Panthers were nabbed by the marine police gave out most of the information. Their financier was a governor in mongalao and a high ranking official, Marseille or the scarlet jaguar.

Deveraux had done his work it was up to Interpol to deal with it, up to this lead Vangezi family was satisfied. Somewhere in the hidden places in Geovis city sat Victor Marcelo's Ban chili. He was smiling about the whole drama that he had masterminded, Jack Marseille A.K.A the scarlet jaguar. That's how the Panthers knew him no one knew the true identity of the financier. He watched as Deveraux and his counterparts played their little game. Gwani that piece of scum let his mouth blubber stuff he doesn't know will cost him, Ban chili swore under his breath. Or maybe he wants to try the dance of death, or head and shoulders it will be. Eventually, Vaza Gwani lost the use of his right limbs caused by gunshots in Geovis state prison.

Someone knew who the scarlet jaguar was and all the details but they feared being silenced in cold blood. Vangezi remained at large and eventually, the Panthers sent a message. A beheaded body of a marine police officer then they called for Vangezi's ransom. The situation was getting ugly and the Panthers were calling for a tough game.

The Panthers had hit the hornets' nest soon or later they would face the sting. The authorities and the marine police had some leads from the Vangezi case all they needed now was leverage. One weekend they geared up for the crackdown, they had turned one of the Panthers to be their state witness. His name was Spike Vangalu. There was a private party as usual 2-kilometers from the crustaceans and 30 km from the mainland.

When the marine police and the paramilitary Special Forces moved in they headed to the cruise liner the crystal sapphire. They jumped on to the cruise liner fired tear gas canisters then sounded the warning. As they crawled in the people scampered in all directions. Spike hinted at them that Vangezi was one deck below. At the end of the hallway with red lights. Somehow Deveraux managed to get himself a paramilitary silver black and green combat. Then came the exchange of gunfire with different war cries, even ground rocket launchers blew up, the condors were part of the fireworks party. The marine cops and the Special Forces were not stupid. They counter-attacked the ship with their best men.

The only one-speed boat escaped with the European millionaire on it. The rest of the condors and the Panthers were cornered. From 100 only 78 were caught the rest of them were turned in to Swiss cheese. They were boats ready to take them back to shore. Deveraux headed down the third deck and then the hallway. The last compartment was where Vangezi was being held, hostage. Marx Deveraux only had one thing on his mind to get his old glory back. He tip toped carefully when he was close enough he shot the lock off then kicked the door.

He was startled what he found the governor in a black and red guerilla combat one arm around Vangezi's neck. Now easy gov you don't want the situation to get any ugly than it is now. Shut up Marx sonny boy if you jackals hadn't ruined my plans I was going to be defense minister. I knew your every move Deveraux, heaved Marcelos as he continued to aim his machine gun at him. This idiot Jerry knew too much so happened the disappearing act chuckled Marcelo's. Game over big bad wolf give up surrender gov, general J. scarlet you wild jackal retorted Marcelos. Vangezi hit marcelos in the ribs with his head he staggered and kicked vangezi who yelled unprintables. He also sent a tirade of bullets in Deveraux direction who dived for cover then sent a volley in Marcelo's direction. He bruised him on the shoulder.

Marcelos had also hit Deveraux in the shoulder, Marcelos groaned Marx you thieving wild dog. I swear I will get you for this you!!!!. Deveraux shifted behind some boxes, hey old wolf I know who you are now. So just give up those pseudo names won't help you red or scarlet (pussycat)Jaguar, Jack Marseille, rubbish! Victor Marcelos Banchili, Deveraux stood up with his assault rifle aimed at Marcelos. Before Marcelos could make a move Vangezi hit Marcelos in the back with an iron bar. Then Deveraux moved swiftly gave Marcelos a sharp kick to the ribs who fell like a log. Can you make it to the rescue boat Vangezi waved Marx, Jerry nodded. Marx fastened his weapon to his right shoulder then swung unconscious Marcelos over the left shoulder. He then headed for the first deck with vangezi ahead of him. When they reached the boat the marine police helped Vangezi get into the boat. Then they got Marcelos and Deveraux into the boat. The police medics wrapped Deveraux's shoulder and patched up Marcelos although he was still unconscious; then headed for the mainland.

Three months later Vangezi was made governor of Geovis city and Marx Deveraux made his glory break but declined to be made the chief of police. He just requested a marine police post be made 100m from shore on the serene islands. Victor Marcelos Banchili was tried and convicted along with the 78 condors and panthers. On the counts of extortion, abduction, money laundering, and another lot more charges. Banchili got 45 yrs and the rest 15 yrs each.

There's your story reporters said Vangalu. Jake and I were more than pleased about our source from inner Mongalao. Who we had paid handsomely. We left on the third day from vangolezi the border town of Mongalao and Zionde our country. We both agreed that if we were permitted to publish it in the Montage.

We were relaxing one Saturday afternoon. Then Jake began a conversation. Michael," I have a little confession to make". Well go on I urged. You remember the time we were covering the mongalao story. Yes, what about it? Mmmmh on the day of the crackdown I was with the Interpol. What!!!!! before he could even finish what he was saying. I was already out of my easy chair for a few minutes. I felt like pumping some sense into Jake's head. What on earth were you thinking and all this time you just kept quiet? Damn you, Jake, you could have gotten yourself killed for what a mega-story? Well, well, well chuckled Jake," so Mr reporter how do you think we got the best shot". Connections huh? The situation was getting a little tense so I just got up.

I think am going to take a walk and get some fresh air. Come on Michael, "am sorry I was going to tell you". Michael put up his hands I give up. But I still need that walk then we can talk about this later ok. After the stroll, I decided to buy a six-pack of mullers lager. I came back to the flat around 18:00hrs. It was kind of funny at 27 we were sharing a three-bedroomed flat.

Right, I feel much better now can we talk this out, Jake? Alright, boss joked Jake, "you kind of overreacted. The locals said, "the authorities in mongalao didn't want any licks". So I decided to take the risk at least I wasn't that close to the cruise liner when the guns went off". We were stationed 100 yards away. Who's we inquired Michael? Spike Vangalu and the Interpol contact Mario Steriaki. So by the time, we were talking to Spike in police custody. It was just protocol I already had what I wanted. Besides, it was your idea that we should go to the damn country for a vacation. Now, what do I get a lecture from you? My apologies Jake I didn't know you went that far to bring closer some big fish. Phew!!!!! Sighed Jake we can both forgive each other break. One more thing Jake yes, I smacked hard on the stomach. He screamed what's that for. Michael chuckled for leaving me behind when I also needed those thrills you felt near the crustaceans.

I think we can cool our selves with muller's lager. About the time where's the party? Michael threw his friend three canned beers.

On Monday morning it was quite a busy day. Michael and Jake were in the reporter's office and thinking about how they can get their big break story published." Well, how are we going to convince Mr. Ngwiza about our big fish". "Remember the mongalao authorities that Dmitri Vangolessi ranting threats, if ever we leaked our source of information from the mongalao foreign press"." Laughed Jake and then he raised an eyebrow and nudged his friend", oh I remember that big punk full of attitude presidential attache' said Michael"." As they were talking the phone rang Michael put his hand up Jake shhhh! Yes, 245 lanski drive got it.

Who was that? Some cop at a murder scene asking if we could go over for some details. Anyway, let's go and see Mr. Ngwiza," you mean the chief editor? Yes agreed on Michael, the chief editor". Is there a problem?" There is something you should know that I should have told you a long time ago", That call from the cop what are the details, well he says the ex-governor of Mongalao's ex-girlfriend is dead it is a horrible scene". "Does this have any connections with what you want to disclose", Michael leaned forward. "Jake began his narration about his childhood and his estranged sister, as well as her connections to high powered officials during her college years. Then there was her sudden disappearance. The rest is history so that address 245 lanski drive rings a bell. "She is my long-gone sister Mike, what exclaimed Michael! You can't be serious". Do I look like I am joking to you, yelled Jake with tears streaming down his face? I am a sorry man but you should have told me, "I am sorry. He hugged his friend close and rubbed his back, now pull your self together then we can go and see Mr. Ngwiza. In his office maybe he can scare the socks off your feet with his bellowing.

Jake wiped his face and straightened his tie. "Well let's go listen to the ranting of the big boss. There were now walking briskly to the chief editor's office and when they reached the office they both heaved. Jake knocked repeatedly at the door, they heard the editor saying come in.

How can I be of help? gentlemen make your selves comfortable he gestured". They sat down usually Michael always spoke for the two of them when there were at the Montage. In the field, Jake took over the spokesman's issues. "Sir we need your approval for the publishing of the story of the Mongalao fiasco. Okay, now circus clowns don't come in here with your little plea of wanting your circus game on the front page of my paper. "We don't understand sir circus games what do you imply? Oh is that so! well, Chingu how do you explain this? He threw a Mongalao private paper with Jake, Steriaki and Spike Vangalu on it. Michael winced and clenched his fist, then Jake propped himself up fixing his eyes on the chief editor.

"Sir, first of all, that image isn't showing what exactly happened, before he could finish he was cut short." Let me warn you these monkey tricks you and your clown friend want to pull won't work so cut to the chase". "Fumed Mr. Ngwiza is that clear? "Yes, sir replied Michael and Jake. Jake cleared his throat, "Sir I don't know where you got that piece of malicious newspaper, but the truth is that the place wasn't an illegal arms sales point"." It was an old warehouse and those two aren't low life scum as the paper puts it, one's Interpol and the other is a state witness.

Chapter Three

An Old Trail

The editor was the one leaning now caught off guard because he had raised some tension, he was now tasting his own medicine. "He turned to Michael, Fwando let's set the record straight this Mongalao nonsense, make me understand how true is the story".

Michael reached into his leather jacket's inner pocket and pulled out a business card." Dmitri Vangolessi Mongalao foreign press attache', call him if you think we are lying". Shortly there was a buzz on the other end of the line. "Vangolessi here who's this?"Ngwiza chief editor Montage newspaper sing a lullaby," Dmitri if you may am listening!!! Chit chat with a stranger huh get to the point, will you?

Well let me roll the wheel like this, is it true some governor ended as garbage over his dirty linen? "on the other end there was silence then Dmitri spoke. 'I don't know where you are getting this trash but between you and me it is true". "Mr. Ngwiza, "yes replied the editor". "Tell your boys Fwando and Chingu next time they hook me up to unexpected they will be flogged when they enter Mongalao ". "The editor heaved cleared his throat and bellowed down his receiver. "Now listen Vangoliz or whatever your name is! This is a direct insult to me and next time you want to chicken shit me think twice". "Dmitri hit back hey wiz porkchop, listen up I meant to warn them about what they should stay away from".

"Fair game captain Rushmore did I ever tell you that I like Russian names, like the French, say au revoir monsieur Vangolessi". With that, the editor put down his receiver. He was looking at his reporters now, well circus clowns looks like your word is the truth". "I don't understand one thing why did you two meddle in a dangerous game like this one?

Michael sat up sir," we are reporters that's what we do, not even landmines can stop us if we are authorized". "I see, daredevils is that what you mean? Sort of, but we need assurance from you and backing". "Only on one condition gentlemen, you tell, me what you will be doing when, where and how?" Are we clear? yes, sir.

By midday the second-page headlines read in part, MONGALAO GOVERNOR TURNS OUT TO BE CRIME BOSS. Everybody at the montage offices applauded Michael and Jake on their achievement. "Hey, Michael 245 lanski we need to be there remember that call? In about an hour there were at the crime scene, who's Chingu? I am," come over said a police detective" You can have this but don't tell anyone I gave you this little book". Giving him a small diary with photos and information on it. As for the body, it's too morbid for you to see let the medical people patch her up.

Within two weeks they buried Jake's sister and every other family member dispersed. It wasn't easy for Jake to get over the tragedy. Though he recovered after a month and some weeks.

One evening after work they were relaxing and eating nuts. Jake began to study the diary from the crime scene and tried his best to concentrate. He stood up paced up and down.

Michael looked at his friend and said," what's the matter anything wrong? Yes, the editor was right we shouldn't have gone too far". What do you mean buddy? "The Panthers and condors are just the icings of the cake, there are the golden wolves of prukianisi and fourth connexion.

"Yes, the whole thing is crumbling, Michael and I am scared". "According to this book, the fourth connexion is second to the golden wolves of prukianisi." Stanley Banchili was once my sister's boyfriend then they broke up". "Stanley is the second in command in the fourth connexion mercenaries".

"Rachel Virginia Chingu became engaged to another man, who was a businessman". "On one of his journeys he ran into Stan and he was detained". "Rachel found out she went to Mongalao press her fiancé was released". "However he didn't last long he was murdered and Rachel was framed"." Until now she had gone into hiding. "The older Banchili had dated my sister before she met Stan who rolled out of state intelligence school because of misconduct". "Stanley has always been shielded by his brother and I know he's responsible for her death".

"Michael, I need your help and we have to be discreet, I am in deep trouble". "Alright, Jake where do I fit into this family debacle? "You watch my back that's how you fit in! "Tell me more about the fourth connexion and golden wolves of prukianisi".

"Andries stanislov Vlad an ex-Russian colonel runs the fourth connexion mercenaries". "If you remember the crustacean issue those Europeans who escaped?"Yes, I do say Michael you mean the mysterious European? "Now you remember I see! What's his name? Jake, Michael motioned with his hand".

"Mario Giovanni Cavali is the golden wolves founder an ex-guerrilla general in the Wangoto Islands"."He also topped the list of the European most wanted crime barons". "So we are not only dealing with the Banchili's but an army of outlaws".

"They are coming after me, I am finished if word of this diary leaks to the press" Jake, your secret is safe with me beside you are my brother and I won't let you down". "Whoever is after you have me to face also". Did I ever tell you about Vasco Mbangeni?

No, anything important about that name? Yes, Vasco is an ex-military man of African European descent". He's related to Marx Deveraux the private investigator who busted the Panthers and Victor Marcelos Banchili on the crystal sapphire".

What's the crystal sapphire? It's a cruise liner owned by Vangezi's business associates the Gustav brothers". Have you forgotten the whole thing, Jake? don't stress too much or you will have a nervous breakdown". "Take a break, Michael took the diary from his friend. Then he gestured him to his bedroom and said, "sleep tight and sweet dreams, buddy".

During the rest of the week, the two reporters worked around the clock. When one of them wasn't in the office the other one was looking for information from the internet about the 4th connexion and golden wolves of prukianisi. Now that they knew what was coming after them, it was high time they got prepared. All they had to do was to keep their investigations off the books.

As the situation was Stanley Banchili didn't even know sweet Virgie had a brother. She had told him her family had died when she was a child and that her only brother was dead. So Jake didn't exist as far as the Banchili's knew he had died at the age of 15.

The detective had told Jake all this but asked him to be discreet about the information. Whoever had been assigned to find Jake was either friend or foe. At least the detective wasn't an enemy but soon or later the others would know that he was alive. This simply showed that they had to move fast.

On a Friday morning, Jake was busy preparing the paperwork from the trainee reporters. Which needed to be taken to the chief editor for assessment. Then the phone rang on the other end some muttering of words was heard. "You what? You have found the rest of the puzzle perfect! "Alright meet me at the canteen in 10 minutes"." I owe you one Michael, said Jake as he put the receiver down". A smile now appeared on his face, the Banchili's had done enough damage now they were going to have payback time.

Somewhere deep in Mongalao trouble was brewing, Stanley was bent on revenge and everybody involved for Victor's imprisonment; was going to pay. To get victor out after he had served 10 years, Stanley was supposed to get rid of all the obstacles to plans. The list was long but at least Virginia was history, Deveraux and the others had to be eliminated. There was a book and photos with incriminating evidence which could bring down the 4th connexion and the prukianisi empire. This was bad as business and power no longer existed and the last thing to happen was going to be a chain reaction. Which was what Stanley didn't want happening because Vlad and Cavali would be caught in a fight. With no more fourth connexion and prukianisi wolves, Stanley would rot in jail for his atrocities.

On the other hand, Marx Deveraux also wanted justice his best friend was shot by the Panthers. It wasn't strange as to why Marx had agreed to investigate Vangezi's disappearance. Now all he needed was the coded diary then the guerillas would go down in flames. Vasco had Marx at one time met and told him about how he could get the coded diary.

Zionde was just the country within arms reach, but it wasn't going to be easy to take out a huge syndicate. No matter what happened the Panthers were going to pay one way or the other. Jake Fwando and Marx Deveraux had almost the same story.

Fate can take it's course sometimes their worlds would meet someday. Before the Vangezi investigation, Marx had pursued a couple of thugs on high way T47. In the process, Deveraux's partner Jacques Sbelo was shot and died from a gunshot wound. On the way to the hospital, Marx found out his assailants' identity.

Shortly the Mongalao papers reported on something concerning a missing governor. The Vangezi family wanted an investigator and here was the chance for Marx: to avenge his friend's murder. He spoke to the family spokesperson and they agreed on the terms that at least he would find out

Chapter Four

Cracking The Puzzle

Vangezi' whereabouts. Marx wasn't too sure on how to approach the matter, because of Jerry Vangezi and his business with outlaws.

The truth of the matter Jerry wasn't gothic or a savage but his clients were a bit unrefined. The story was that Jerry owned a yacht. The Gustav brothers had joint business with him, there was however one bizarre thing on the cruise liner. Every mid-month PTS and CDS associates had meetings on the Cruise liner which didn't cater for the press except on rare occasions.

All this had come to light when Marx was investigating the nature of the disappearance. Somewhere somehow somebody was going to sing. Panthers and condors were smaller cells of the golden wolves of prukianisi and 4th connexion, as Marx had come to learn.

It wasn't going to be long before PTS and CDS would have their pants down and everybody watching their dirty deeds. Just like coincidence when the catastrophe struck there was one reporter who resembled Virgie R. Chingu from Zionde. Though he had come and gone out of mongalao Marx had noticed him. So when Victor Banchili had been jailed, the story of a woman murdered in the neighboring country had tongues wagging.

The pieces of the puzzle were falling into place so Marx was sticking them together. Apart from that, he knew he was being followed and somebody wanted him dead. The moment Victor Banchili had gone behind bars, as Spike had told him about Stanley Banchili and his part in the Panthers. The closest description of Stanley was a large scar on the back of his neck and a missing thumb.

As for the rest of the information he couldn't get it. Spike was found dead at his flat with a heavily bruised neck, made by something coarse like barbed wire. Marx figured one thing though Stanley's thumb had been replaced by a metallic thumb. Which he could use on his victims with the very little swing of power.

An ex-military man who had served in the gulf war wouldn't end up like a chicken or rabbit Marx had kept a low profile about his past life. He just served as a police detective and private investigator for the past 35 years. Until now he was going to use his army instincts to bring down his stalker and some dirty mercenaries. These had been terrorizing the coastal town of Mondo.

First things first Deveruax knew someone wanted him dead but who was it? Marx had only one way to find out how to get the coded diary. One morning he dialed an international number at the other end a voice spoke up.

"Yes, Vasco here," Deveraux old cousin how's the food in Zionde. Huh! Marx still pretending to be a cop, I think you miss the army". "Don't be naïve Vasco am done running and dodging flying debris". "Well, sing you haven't phoned me in a long time, what's up to anything new?

"You are right, am looking for someone very important, does the name chingu mean anything to you?" Go on said, Vasco the name may ring a bell". Did you know a Virginia Fwando who has murdered three months ago, Marx? "You mean the governor's former mistress, "yes what about her?

"Come on Vasco can't you read between the lines?" Five years ago Virginia was done with the Banchili's, during the same years she got engaged". To whom did she get engaged? Arthur Sbelo my partner's half brother' you are joking, right? ' No Vasco I wish I was, there is more to it'.

'Keep talking am all ears', alright then before they could officially marry Arthur Sbelo brother was found dead at his flat'. 'Virginia Chingu was framed for the murder with her fingers prints all over the crime scene'.' I think the Banchili's wanted her to keep her mouth shut for a long time'.

'I am lost Marx but why? 'Do you think she had information about their dirty deeds? ' You mean mercenaries business how did you know about that?' I may not be a cop but I have connections the Banchili's are real vermin". ' I know at least something about them' okay now listen Vasco do you remember Vangalu?

'Yes, why do you ask? ' He was murdered after he had given me a description of Stanley Banchili; his scars around the neck matched those on Anthony's body and Virginia's too. ' Except for one thing Virginia had the word traitor branded on her back'. ' Marx that's inhumane and who do you think is behind those diabolical murders? ' I am not sure but Virginia's brother may be alive and I want you to find him'. ' Marx Deveraux,'you are becoming obsessed with this thing, if I may ask what makes you think he's alive?

'Please Vasco it's important don't be a fool, you and I both know, that Virginia's brother is at risk'.' He is the next target so be careful'. 'what makes you so sure?' Virginia had a diary nicked from Stanley Banchili and it was missing at the crime scene'. ' It had all leads on the mercenaries and my good friend Mario Zinde was around that scene'. ' I suspect he gave it someone it belonged to though I can't tell how the assassin failed to find it'.

'The chances are there is a Chingu alive and you should get to him first before the Banchili's barbeque him'.' What job would he be doing? ' A reporter maybe, I don't know? just find him alright, yelled Marx'. ' Okay but you sound like you are working for someone, Marx tells me the truth!

What's going on even if I knew the whereabouts of Virginia Chingu's brother, I need the truth first.' Okay am sorry but I think you need to come Fire blossom resort on phone I can't say everything'. ' Professor truth I think you are nuts am not a sell-out, see you soon'.

'Vasco Mbangeni chuckled,' adios student crazy cop and he hangs up'.

It had been a week since Jake and Michael had been working at finding the facts about the mercenaries. After rummaging through Interpol files provided by detective Zinde, they had found something a coded folder with six figures in it. There six people in small pictures with profiles about them and information concerning their crimes.

The key to the whole puzzle was the diary as it once belonged to Stanley Banchili. It contained account numbers of the fourth connexion and golden wolves. As well as hideouts and plans of the mercenaries to take over Bamvunde a small country which was an island. Near Mongalao with oil fields and some gold in it.

The coded folder had three familiar faces Victor, Stanley, and Marco Da Silva. In two hours the guys had been done. They got back at the Montage and the editor's secretary beckoned them to his office. When they got in the spun around in his office chair.

'Tell me something circus clowns what have you two been up to? ' Nothing sir, just relaxing'. Oh is that so, someone said you two have been snooping around the police station lately'. ' I hope there isn't anything stupid you are planning to do after losing your sister Chingu? ' No sir we just wanted to confirm a case of a robbery reported around the area'.

'I see since when did you start paying courtesy calls to the Zionde police'. Every time we have duty calls sir' is there a problem? No boys just checking to make sure that you don't catch me off guard' you can go.

Buzz, buzz yes my friend what are you up to this time? Nothing, listen jack 1 whatever you and your friends are doing, do it fast and don't forget to be careful!

Then the line went dead."Vasco, Vasco……? Since then there was no communication, jack figured out one thing trust was becoming a rare treat.

The two reporters were busy working their way through the puzzle. Bee sting or Stanley bent on revenge and the golden wolves and fourth connexion heat up for a coup. Everybody going in circles the chase had just begun.

"Michael I now know why the book was treasure, it's all here operation jivundu. It's a coup plan with leaders but without the banchili's it can't work"." It seems we have our puzzle cracked after all" Well my friend what do you think? "We should quit being reporters hey?

"Very funny you bet your fortune on that one, Jake!

Michael looked at the maze they had created in the warehouse from their visit to Mongalao: to Spike's disappearance. Everything they had come in contact with recently and the result? It was a small world war.

Chapter Five

The Final Score

"**M**ichael, are you even listening to me? "I thought I had answered your questions?

"Sorry, what were you saying? Never said 'I wanted to tell you that we need a back plan'If Ngwiza ever finds out we are toasted, worse more fired; Jake don't fidget, I think he already knows about this debacle.

"If you say so, well I was saying we have found that all the other things were decoys all along these mercenaries had been planning for a coup de'tat on Bamvunde"

"It's goldmines, oil, and gas. Power! That's what they wanted power.' These six figures Marcelos, Stan, Vlad, Cavalli, Gustav, and Maza de langelo, are the operation jivundu. They planned everything but Da Silva Alias Zinde was smart.

"Phew!!!!!! Look Michael said, "to his friend." I know this is driving you crazy but we need a break" Is that okay? No problem at that point they left as the room. As the warehouse could be hot sometimes.

Vasco Vincent Mbangeni, a coloured born from an Italian father and an African mother. Drilled to be what he was, later found out he had a brother in Africa. He was in the army by then and had made friends with Jack Deveraux. He had tried to locate his brother but to no avail.

It had taken six years, then in the sixth, he was framed the case was that. he was involved with mercenaries.

Andries Stanislov Vlad and his minions were responsible. After the catastrophe had died down. Vasco applied for retirement. When it couldn't work, he arranged one by beating his drill sergeant. He was sent home for disciplinary action. He weaved a story about an accident.

In which he had died then changed his name Vincente de Silverio to Vasco Vincent and Mbangeni from his mother. 15 years later after he had met Michael. Then he went into hibernation. But he had received information that he was free.

Until now after his phone call with Michael, he sent an e-mail to him. Which read.......

How are you, brother?

I know you are annoyed, I wasn't there as a brother. But don't worry I have been watching you. Right here in Zionde, I am in a position that is compromised. If I get to you then your friend will in a tight spot. I have reservations for things that should have done in a long time, only time and space could allow. But I think we had to get the banchili's first. When this is over.

We can be brothers the way we should have been years ago. The Vercetti,s can go to hell as I wasn't their puppet. So take care of Jake. Cover your tracks by taking a vacation with your friend. So you can find out some horrible truth about Mongalao's underground operations.

Nzinzi island is the best place, for now, there are no snitches. Make sure you are not followed.

Love Vincente Mbangeni

Michael sat looking at the monitor of the home computer. Then looked around the posh flat they share with Jake. A dream had come half true.

This was all because of Virginia Chingu's antics with the mercenary big shots. Then Jake called Michael, "hey what was it you were saying?

"I am lost in translation, refresh my memory"You were saying something about Ngwiza, "Yes what about Ngwiza?

"Oh don't get excited,'Ngwiza is former intelligence he has his ears to the ground"You mean he knows about this rendezvous, "You are right, General!

"So the rest of the depart is in the dark about our little game". Then Jake opened his eyes wide and there was a broad grin on his face. Just the look in his eyes could show trouble was brewing behind his eyes. Michael snapped his fingers and waved his hands in front of him.

"Hey, man what are you up to? You look dubious, what's on your mind charm" He chuckled a little, then turned to his friend."Michael, are you thinking what I am thinking?

"What, I don't know tell me"We can always choose the less of two evils" wait a minute, Jake you mean using all our contacts, even the vile ones? To the point and precise Yes! Michael shifted about in his seat, then he beckoned his friend to the computer.

"Read the last paragraphs of the email, I received from Vasco" What do I look like I need babysitting," he yelled! Shhhh! Calm down my friend the Banchili's may be malicious as El Diablo, but they are also cunning as foxes".

"What does the Spanish word mean?' The Devil, now listen my brother has a lot he wants to say but not around this town".' Then where does he want to spill his beans?'Nzinzi island in two weeks "You are not planning to do me over, are you Michael? Tell me, I don't know whom to trust now?

"Certainly not as Michael stood up, with his face close to his friend's face, I know you are in a bad situation", Read the rest of the e-mail and tell me if I am hiding something".Jake scrolled the remainder of the paragraphs, then checked the source of the e-mail. To his surprise, it was coded and the name Vincente bothered him.

"Michael who is Vincente? This time the bravado and colour had faded from his face." My brother's real name is Vincente de Silverio Mbangeni, my mother's maiden name"He was born before she married my father", Vasco was framed for selling arms to mercenaries on Italian soil"

"He traced his real family, me' he was court marshaled and lost his rank as captain"To prove his point after they denied retirement' He broke the drill sergeant's jaw

"What happened then? This time Jake was beaming and pumped up with pride."He faked his death in a dummy accident and changed his name".' He's been around Mongalan borders and in Zionde". 'Just like you he's my estranged brother, Jake!

"I am sorry, Michael' for not trusting you", The pot calls the kettle black, "Jake thrust his hand bygones partner? Michael caught him and spun him in a judo spin but shielded him with his leg." Bygones welcome to camp firefly 'frowning Jake swept him with his left leg. Both on the floor.

They lay laughing then there was a buzz on the doorbell.

Michael got up "I will get it when he opened the door he saw Mr. Ngwiza" Surprised to see me, circus clown? You look as if you have seen a ghost!' Where's your psycho friend Chingu?

Jake frowned" I heard that wiz pork chop! What you hotheaded imbecile' come here so I can teach you some manners! Bring it on Grandpa retorted Jake'

"Hey, Gabriel!!! yelled, Michael stop it! And say why you are here; holding his arms and pushing him aside. Fine Fwando but don't call me by my first name"I will if you don't behave, said Michael.

"Well if you recall your rendezvous in Mongalao, Stanley Banchili wanted Spike Vangalu dead. 'Yes go on urged Jake'Ngwiza raised an eyebrow then continued, "Spike Vangalu Ngwiza is alive because Stanley thought he is you, Michael" A tourist but I know Jake you may be thinking of getting the banchili's, let the law take its course"

"If I may ask and why's that Mr. Ngwiza?Because they are mercenaries and dangerous who want to keep things secret"Gentlemen' I am leaving."

Michael walked him to the door "Goodnight Sir, so long Mike". When he was out of earshot Jake quizzed" Michael do you think Ngwiza is telling the truth or playing us with his gasbag tactics?

"I don't know Jake but we will find out soon, we will find out soon……..

"Mr. Fwando's office how can I help you?" I want to speak to Michael "Sorry call back in five minutes he will be back by then" Alright tell him I called'. I will do the honors, Geraldine smiled to herself.

Geraldine had been working for the Montage newspaper for a long time now. She liked Michael Fwando from the day he had set foot in the offices.

About fifteen minutes later, Michael stormed into the offices looking exhausted. Geraldine looked from her computer"Hey charm boy!charm boy quizzed Michael."Geraldine smiled"No I meant Michael there was a call for you before you came in"

'Who was on the line?' I don't know to check your answering machine! Mike yes, Gera what's up? Do you have a minute? Make it quick, turned to face her' You wouldn't mind joining me for lunch, would you?'No, which the place do you have in mind?'La Roche' café 1 o clock"

"Alright then consider it done".

Michael proceeded to his office, then pressed a button on the answering machine."Yes, little Mike or my loud Mike.' I hope you and your clown friend aren't planning any pranks on me." 'Well like I said I want you and your friend to come to the island as planned' 'don't draw any attention, just normal vacation". "By the way, I 've'got some hot little mama's I would like you to meet"Chiao Mike"

Michael laughed a little then dialed an international number"Buzz, Buzz then a voice muttered on the other end ....' Did you listen to my little proposal little brother? You are crazy Vasco I don't do escorts"Scared of a little foreplay tiger?' Be a man mommy won't wack you?' What are you up to, buying me a Japanese geisha?'Chill, kiddo just do what you do best play soldier"

"Vasco, don't start with me','Michael have you told your friend about your army rendezvous? Before you answer like you exposed my moonlighting with Gisele", Alright, alright you mean my stint with Valerie Lucille the sergeant.' 'Yeah go on kiddo 'I will tell him my self!

"Anything else?' No kiddo you tell me ' Ngwiza sung says Spike Vangalu is his boy; do you think he's working for the banchili's? "I don't know Mike but I have got a dossier on him, wait I will call you back soon"

Hello, Mike he's clean but watch your backs! Cheers Vincent, "right see you kiddo"

"Suddenly Jake stormed in, in hand, in hand with Roselyn Stamos; Roselyn was in the foreign news department. Jake looked rosy-cheeked.

Michael chuckled, "Well, well I pronounce you husband and wife 'love birds'.Roselyn, blushed, Michael why do you torment Jake" 'He just swept me like a hurricane about your Mongalao adventures".

Michael raised his eyebrows, "Oh really, by charming you? Mike don't start I know about your Varie Lucille Vlashiknov" 'Michael opened his lips but he was speechless and a little purple in his face. Fuming," he ranted, Vasco never learns to keep his mouth shut, damn him!!!!

"I was only joking"Turning to Michael with wink'friends again", Alright then, as he shook Jake's hand, he checked the watch."I am running late! Feigning surprise Roselyn blocked his way," What about the adventure story?"' I was only an accomplice, Jake is the mastermind, didn't you mention that eee? No, anyway where are you rushing to? quizzed Jake'

"Lunch with Geraldine Nayankis at La Roche' café 1 o clock! Jake grinned and laughed, de Ja !!! Michael finished it off de Ja Vu' in one day! With that, he winked Roselyn," Take care of him he likes getting into trouble"He weaved his way out and he was gone.

"So you told me Michael is the main character in your adventures but it's you who's the big shark, am I right?" Yes, Jake replied in a low tone"

"Are there some loose ends you need to tie or it was just baiting?" Come on Roselyn bait for what?'You know am not sixteen any more? So what? Roselyn closed the door and wrapped her hands around his neck.

"Rose please shall I finish the story about Mongalao?'You will do that later right now fight me tiger"Before Jake could say anything, she covered his mouth with hers and kissed him for a long time". Then let go a little unwrapping her hands. She beckoned him with a finger, then whispered how about power rush"what are you out of your mind? We get our selves fired for gross misconduct.

"Jake shhhh!!!My place today is our scheduled day, come on"You little devil, alright"He scribbled a little note for Michael indicating that he shouldn't wait as he goes home a little late.

Jake picked up a file on desk cleared his throat then said, "Jacques, "Yes sir tell Mr. Ngwiza that we are going to some real mess in a residential area"What else? Roselyn is accompanying me and a report will be ready on Wednesday morning"

"Mr. Chingu how about my columns on the sports page?"Consider it approved, Jake gave him a come ain't done here glance." Thanks, sir, see you Wednesday morning." I don't like Jacques he seems nosy"Roselyn,' he's the best recruit he covers for Michael and me,' besides he's discreet and loyal" 'Okay shall we get to my flat fast, I don't want to spoil my fun"

Michael ate his spaghetti hungrily, Geraldine was staring at him. He looked up"hey your food is getting cold, Geraldine." Oh silly me, she stuffed her mouth with a meatball then washed it down with a soda drink.

"So why did you bring me out here? Geraldine smiled" well there's somebody who likes you and wants to know you better"Yes go on," let's just say she thinks you might turn her down" 'Really what makes think like that?

"I don't know recently you seem withdrawn, this Vasco is keeping you on your toes?" Michael looked away and frowned, look get to the point?" That Vasco is my estranged brother and breathes this to Ngwiza, you will regret it" 'I am sorry Michael I didn't mean that……..!" Alright, Geraldine, I can't help thinking this secret admirer is you!

Geraldine coughed then said," what Mike me? Yes, this time Michael looked at her straight in the eyes." Tell me how long have you been spying on me? Mike I can explain" Michael motioned the waiter and paid the bill.

"Geraldine we are leaving" 'Michael I haven't even touched my food yet, are you mad at me?' Yes I am now come on let's go"

Geraldine obeyed nervously following. After heaving a lot Michael turned to her, "look I am sorry if embarrassed you at la Roche' café. 'You are right it's the Mongalao issue and not Vasco, which is driving me crazy"

In a low voice Geraldine," said am I forgiven for spying on you? Yes, we all make mistakes Gera. Michael felt bad when he realized she was crying." Hey, what can I do to make you feel better? 'Hug me, smiled Geraldine.

He gave her a bear hug, "Alright I know you like me and I have been too blind to see that, tell me since when? Geraldine opened her purse then gave him a photo of an old man. In the sixties or so.

"Does he ring a bell? Michael shook his head Bindwo, no this can't be ", 'Yes it is, she showed him some evidence of him being alive. I thought he had died in a car accident.

"How do you think I got my job at the Montage?"If you know him this much are you related? I am his only daughter" "Geraldine I will be honest, I need some time when we get to know each other better" "if you say so', one thing baffles me dad never told me about your fiery temper"

"You caught me by surprise" He then hailed a taxi for her, see you later sugar. She turned and kissed him on his lips, "goodbye love"

As she got into the cab she blew him a kiss.

Suddenly his phone rung Ngwiza was on the line."Hey, circus clown where are you right now drinking your head off?' No potato pie! 'What you!!!! 'I mean am eating it's lunchtime remember?' Oh, you got, sorry but you better be here in 10minutes" 'Alright chief' Michael cut the call.

He thought for a while then laughed. If Bindwo was alive then Geraldine's work as a secretary was just a cover-up. Bindwo had him hooked all along, his price for mentoring him. Geraldine was a sweet person and whatever would happen then! She would run to daddy and hell would break loose. At least he knew where they stood 'quicksand'. He got on a cab and went straight to Montage offices.

In Mr. Ngwiza's office, Sir, "you wanted to see me".Yes, he spun in his chair to face him. What's this letter doing on my desk"You mean the leave request? "Yes, of course, that crap, tell me do I look like a circus master?" Maybe you the one saying it"

"Well, it seems like you have grown wings Fwando", "Really how big are they? Pointing at his back with his thumb.

"Stop playing games with me, what's on Nzinzi Island?"None of your concern but beautiful young ladies!" So you want a short holiday eeeeh?" Yes, sir, "Fwando, if anything goes amiss, call me, "Is that clear?" Why sir? Spike survived because Stanley Banchili thought he was you, a tourist".

"However he isn't coming after you, he just wants to release his brother from jail"

"I see' and you will be updated on any strange happenings". "Now that's a good boy, you can go, I 've' already signed your leave papers, tell your rookie friend it's a done deal"

After the meeting with Ngwiza, Jake phoned to say he would be back by Friday. Michael cursed over the phone because they were falling behind schedule. If they took long going to Nzinzi island Ngwiza's suspicions would now turn into intrigue, which the last thing he wanted happening.

It was Thursday 9;30 in the evening Michael dialed Roselyn's number, Hello Jake? Roselyn yes answered in a whisper tone."Put Jake on the phone now!you little devil" 'Alright don't be sarcastic like you silly friend.

"Hey, buddy how was your date with Geraldine?" Sour and it turns out she is Bindwo's little girl" You are joking" Really am I?

"Jake cook up a story to get Roselyn occupied but be here tomorrow at 10 o clock" 'Mike come Nzinzi op' can't we leave on Saturday?" No bone head we don't want to raise suspicion" Got it? Yeah, boss!

"Jake," Yes Michael "Put Roselyn on the phone" Why? Just do it and be here tomorrow as planned"

"Hey Mike, am...are you planning to spoil my silver rendezvous?"No not all Rosy just wanted to remind Jake about the bills and laundry"Do me a favour don't feed him eels or barbel fish"Why is he afraid of it? 'No allergic dummy!' He is all yours but please let him come home at 9 o clock tomorrow"

"Okay fine by me, by the way, Geraldine is a bit upset" 'What's the reason?' She said you spoiled her lunch break"

"Roselyn, yes Mike" keep your self out this okay"Alright I will but don't hurt Geraldine" The line went dead...Mike? Right 'fire Mike' lights up again" Motioning to Jake: they poured themselves some champagne cuddling and laughing before finally falling asleep.

At 10;00hrs the doorbell rang, Michael was shocked at what he saw. Jake and Roselyn lip-locking it away and Roselyn; still dressed in her nightgown. He pulled them both in.

"Hey the two of you, have you lost your minds? What giggled Roselyn are we embarrassing you?"You are behaving like animals,' separating them." Roselyn how about you go get dressed and see you in a week?" You are nuts, I ain't leaving!" Yes, you are" Mike wait, Jake put up his hand.

"Rosy baby, listen we are running late for a flight, "I have a message on your recorder"

"Jake, what's going? This is bullshit, where are you going? Rose is work-related ' So saying he walked her to the car.

They hugged and Roselyn called Michael, please bring him back to me safely"I will I promise"

"One more thing "And what's that Roselyn? Jake is a missile expect a niece or nephew Mike! What Roselyn are you serious? Then she waved and shouted bon voyage".

"Jake you dodge bone head I was busy strategizing for our Nzinzi vacation; and what were you doing moonlighting with easy Roselyn? What do you want triplets?

"Hold it commander "peeping" Varie Lucille has a daughter who looks like you! So don't lecture me about morals" What do you expect me to do watch you play Casanova? Jake at least let me know which one you are keeping?

"Mike we Nzinzi bound or should I call Roselyn and increase the number of your nieces and nephews?" Alright, alright change into that suit then we are good to go" Why should I look like an accountant? Jake stop fooling around our taxi is already here!

Michael had already packed the suitcases he carried them to the cab. Jake locked the flat and left the keys with the doorman. He later joined his friend in the cab. Then they were racing to the airport, after 45 minutes they were on a private jet.

They flew for 4 hours, the flight attendant announced, "please your seat belts, we will be landing at Nzinzi international airport" 'We hope you have enjoyed the flight and enjoy your holiday on Nzinzi island".

"After landing the two gentlemen were chauffeured in a black Mercedes. They were driven 30 minutes nonstop until they reached the resort. After arriving the bell boy carried their suitcases to the suite 1347. Which was self-contained and with exquisite taste.

"Are you Mbangeni junior and your friend Fontani Nzelo," Aah… Yes, why do you ask? said, "Michael to the waiter." This way Vasco will be joining you shortly, he showed them to a table overlooking the beach.

"Can I take your orders? lobsters, pasta, roast beef, and golden hammer two lagers" 'Alright then by the way my name is Silverio Szutalo" 'Sure thing Silverio, said"Mike faking a smile.

"Phew !!!! Mike am tired, you that "Jetlag eeeh!! Chuckled Michael,' is that the issue?

"No Roselyn she asked me to marry" 'So what are your plans, I said yes" 'What Jake without talking to me first? "I had no choice this Nzinzi flight caught me off guard".

"Do you like her? 'Like you must be nuts I love her" 'Okay Jake, I understand you have been fooling around so it's time right?"You are damn right".

"How about Valerie Lucille Vlashiknov tell me more?"She was a pain the butt" rose in ranks and made me live like a pig"Somebody wanted to torture me, she was sent to my quarters" 'Then what happened?

"We fought I hit her hard thinking she was a man" The fiasco passed but not her injuries" I didn't want the superiors to give me a sentence in military confinement".So Vasco suggested I romance her"Then what was the aim of your rendezvous? 'Erase the pain and before she knew the truth, I would be long gone.

"Well let's enjoy our little holiday" Yeah, you are right," Jake leaned back. Shortly they were into their cuisine dishes. As they ate both were tapped on their shoulders. Michael turned to see a beautiful lady asking him if she could join him, and Jake was asked a similar question.

"It's alright ladies, "Jake should we order some cuisine" Yeah captain smiled Jake" The ladies replied no, we are fine maybe champagne" Jaked chuckled okay senorita's, waiter two bottles chardonnay"

They both finished their meals and lagers.

Michael went first may I know the name of my guest?"Jordy, she smiled shyly"wow you are local here? 'No just touring' 'Now on Jake's part"Does an angel like you have a name?"Nancy, she giggled"Then we are four Romeos and Juliet'

They chatted for long hours and poured champagne laughed and cuddled till late. They drunk their champagne until they were quite tipsy. The ladies left. About an hour Vasco had been watching them through the night scope.

"He smiled and said," welcome boys the fun has just begun, so will the action" Silverio laughed"Your brother seemed apprehensive, you were right he's no dummy" 'So much for the comments make sure my lads are safe" Sure thing boss"

Neither Michael nor Jake knew how they had walked to their rooms. They had walked staggering with Silverio and another room attendant at 3 am and it wasn't long before Saturday morning.

"Wakie, wakie lazy bones" 'What you little chicken don't wake me"Vasco put an ice cube on Michael's face and Mike jumped."Hey can't I get some sleep in this silly resort?"Easy soldier, how are you, little brother?How about a thank you, "Well puppet master am glad to see you"Thank you for pumping me with choke champagne eeeh!Mike keeps it low will you?'

"Sorry, you are awake?"Chingu meets Vasco the "Spook".

"Nice meeting you" Vasco smiled"it's my pleasure"Same as me thanks for the hot lady" 'You are welcome, Mike here doesn't thank me for anything though" 'By the way did Michael finish the story about the Russian lady' 'Yes he did"

"Vasco doesn't start we are not boys anymore" Well, well Michael why don't we get formally introduced?

"Jake," this is my elder brother Vasco Vincent Mbangeni' and Vasco this is my friend Jake Chingu". ' I believe we all know the matter at hand 'Virginia's murder"

Vasco shrugged" hey why don't the two of you get freshened up and meet me at the same bar you went to last night" in about 15 minutes" Jake smiled, "no problem chief, it's a done deal"

Jake and Michael facing Vasco then a platter was brought with cigars on it and glasses. "Vasco," Jake and I don't smoke you know that right? "Take it easy how about pretending, only one is real the other two are plastic" "And why is that? "So nobody will get our attention I will smoking the real one". Then Vasco lit up his cigar and puffed smoke into the air……

Below the cigars were photos and cutouts of information showing the Banchili's and the operation jivundu coup plans. Fourth connexion and Golden wolves of prukianisi. Every incriminating evidence.

"Wow Mike how about we convince Ngwiza he will be glad" 'After what Stan did to Spike he will be fuelled with revenge"

"No Jake can't you see if we publish this we will be hunted and butchered just like the others" So Vasco what's your plan?

"I am going for my revenge on the damned mercenaries" 'As for the two of you go for the Bianchi's, Stan in particular"

"When is that going to happen? Michael asked with a little doubt.

Vasco replied," They are moving Victor Banchili to court on Tuesday, we will be at sea"What happens next? He handed them two small books."Jake if you get the chance shoot, Stan, in the head" 'Alright boys here's the plan" this they spoke in whispers.

After they had finished Vasco sealed the folder and addressed it the Montage newspaper offices. Which he gave to Silverio to mail it immediately. "Boys tonight your hotties are coming" 'What Vasco am not a drunk and Casanova! Complained Michael." Don't worry they won't get pregnant, just a little foreplay to give you fire! Adios

Jake and Michael toured the island and sent e-mails to Mr. Ngwiza; with bikini-clad ladies and the white sand beach with the hot spots plus scenery. In the evening they returned to the resort. This time they were shown to different suites.

Jake entered one scented with jasmine and tulips filled with rosebuds with a Jacuzzi." Am I dreaming? "I think I am Jakes Bond,' from Nzinzi with love" he chuckled. Nancy wearing nothing but stilettos beckoned him with a finger. Obeying he stripped closed the door and tiptoed to the Jacuzzi.

"Michael upon entering just whispered, "just like old days'his suite scented with tulips and lavender, with a steam shower. Jordy popped her head with wet hair and said in a low tone, "afraid of a little foreplay tiger? 'What you little devil this one will tear you to pieces". So saying that he was already in his Adam suit with suite safely locked.

As he got into the shower Jordy teased" growl, growl, growl, grrrrrrrrr!!!

The next day things were a bit different Michael and Jake were summoned. Though this time to a different location. Their one night stands took a flight back to mongalao at 10hrs.

Vasco met Michael and Jake at the oyster Bangalore. Then laid down the master plan on what would be going down on Bamvunde island.

"So boys any one of us who doesn't know how to shoot a gun? "Me, Jake raised his eyebrows."Okay, that will be taken care of" Vasco took them to a shooting range. They did some rounds with a luger, M56 rifle, 9mm Beretta and a Uzzi submachine gun.

"Remember our mission get many pictures and record all you will see you" Stay out of the line of fire" The Banchili's are mercenaries with a quest for Bamvunde"

"Vasco," what's my role in all of this?" Hey little Mike yours is watching your friends back's mean watch your backs"

"Anything else we need to know" He showed them guerilla combat attire and boots." 4 am we leave for Bamvunde,'Deveraux will be joining us"

"Who's Deveraux? Michael asked looking puzzled. Vasco looked him straight in the eye, he's an old friend from my army days" He's clean okay? "Alright, I just wanted to be clear!

At exactly 11 am the phone rung, Mr. Ngwiza was the line. He wanted to talk to Michael. Jake and Vasco told Michael they would wait at port lungelo-marques.

"Hello sir,'Yes circus clown I have got good and bad news" I am all ears boss"

"First of all Spike is undercover but the Banchili's are on Bamvunde, "If you are planning to hit them forget it"The good news is that Spike will deliver everything you want, so be back on Friday"

"How did you find out?" I have got contacts too! Fwando! "Yes, sir" Come back in one piece the both of you". Then there was silence on the line.

Michael had already found out who Silverio was. At the oyster, he looked for him then asked: "where's my brother?" Do you mean Vasco? "Yes, you little skunk do I look like a poker dummy?" Hey easy and don't be rough" They rescheduled, left the port and heading for Bamvunde"

"What on who's the word?" Jake your friend got annoyed when you took that call" It seems you were on the phone for more than half an hour"

"Silverio please tell my brother to take care of Jake and himself"

"What else boss you are in charge now that your brother is away!" Get me to a safe location with communication systems that can connect to Zionde" 'One more thing don't forget to tell me when

Vasco's back" Silverio took him to the vault of high tech gadgets Vasco's lab.

"Silverio smiled, Mike doesn't worry your friend will be okay" So will your brother". At that point, Silverio left and went to the port as instructed.

The 375 horsepower firebird speed boat cruised at top speed towards Bamvunde. By midnight they had crawled into the island. Underdeveloped goldmines, oil fields, and power…... the mercenaries were going to be stopped.

Deveraux, Jake, Vastapos, Vasco, and Inspector Dubois were on the boat with different missions. They reached the coast then hid the boat. They moved in and set camp at an abandoned warehouse.

The house was overlooking the Governor's house in Bamvunde on a hill.

At 9:30 Tuesday cameras were set. At 10:00hrs sharp through binoculars Vasco saw a rocket hit the police headquarters. Then guns started going off. Jake at first was acting as a reporter, though with one eye looking for Stanley Banchili.

The soldiers of bamvunde were good they counter-attacked the Golden wolves mercenaries with the Governor hidden away. Grenades blasting, rifles tearing the air. A helicopter showed up and dropped 10 more mercenaries, this was now war.

"Boys if we have to get out alive let's stick to the guns," said Vasco. They cocked their uzzi's, lugers and assault rifles.

Vasco saw Stan and Vlad fire a missile at the door of the Governor's offices which exploded sending flying debris all over. Then Stan and Vlad stepped in. Vasco nudged Jake "our package is in the bag". Amidst crossfire, they used smoke bombs to get into the Governor's office crawling.

Inside a volley of bullets sent them diving for cover. Vasco shouted," let's take out these pirate lords and feed them to the vultures". 'Jake stay behind me" Jake nodded sure thing General"

Vasco seeking justice, Vastapos and Dubois on the verge of catching international mercenaries. Deveraux with one quest to finish off Banchili scum, same as Jake vengeance.

Rat-at-at-at-ta, boooooooom, bang. The five-hit the red zone when they shot and wounded Vlad and Stan. With the mercenary leaders retreating, Dubois pressed a button on his G.P.R.S which sent a signal to Interpol for back up. In case of trouble was waiting for them at the exit.

Stan didn't want to rot in jail like his brother he took off running. Jake saw him and chased after him. Vasco shouted," Jake noooo! It is a trap you might die in the crossfire. It was too late to warn him.

After pursuing 100yards the shot stan in the shoulder who only staggered. "You fool stop" so I send you to where you belong" Stan shouted you little worm I should have known that you were Deveraux's leverage on my brother's case; I would have butchered you just like Virginia and the rest of the cockroaches" Stan was still moving…..Jake continued chasing. When gunfire from Interpol and 50 of the mercenaries roared up tearing the air. One bullet in the shoulder, leg and the hip. Jake fell yelling "Vasco don't let me die!

Vasco crawled in wearing Interpol combat gear this time while firing at the mercenaries. He pulled Jake to a safe place; Then he dialed his GPRS. "Hey little mike sorry Jake is badly wounded" he was chasing Stan Banchili and got caught in the crossfire"

"Michael was emotional" Vasco bring him back to me do you hear me? Vasco cut the line an Interpol medic moved in and bandaged Jake. Then he was taken to a helicopter waiting which took off instantly with Vasco at the side.

Deveraux had followed Stanley Banchili and shot him in the leg. With Interpol closing in and the army from Bamvunde the mercenaries surrendered. The Banchili's busted forever and Golden wolves dealt with, Deveraux and his men would receive more than a pat on the back.

Jake was flown to Nzinzi island hospital when the chopper landed he was rushed to the emergency room. After a heated argument, Vasco told Michael to call him after a week as Nzinzi operation fire Ant was done Vasco left. Patting his brother on the back "he will be fine don't worry"

With an agitated friend at his side holding him sobbing, "You will be fine after surgery and I will be your best man Roselyn asked me to take you back alive" you will be fine"

With bleeding wounds, Jake narrated the story. The Golden wolves of prukianisi and fourth connexion had failed again.

"Jake I am sorry Ngwiza held me up on the phone I should have been there" The doctors came and wheeled Jake into surgery after an hour a surgeon came told him"Mr. Fwando your friend will be fine.

"This is what happened to the "Operation Jivundu" Jack Marcelos Banchili never got his power instead he saw his downfall.

One year later, at the Montage offices; the Head of foreign news was Jake Chingu and Michael Fwando home news. Vasco Mbangeni Interpol operations commanding officer of Zionde.

Everybody with a bittersweet but happy ending. Deveraux had Stanley and Victor Marcelos Banchili where he wanted them jail rotting for their atrocities.

Roselyn had twins one boy, one girl with Jake after a colourful wedding. Michael got married to Geraldine two months with Bindwo giving her way, it was spectacular.

Every dog has its day in a reporter's world surviving in unfamiliar waters was one thing! The boys had lived their dream.

Lightning Source UK Ltd.
Milton Keynes UK
UKHW021017210820
368606UK00012B/944